LITTLE RED HEN

a faith tale

Story Retold by

BEVERLY CAPPS BURGESS

Illustrations by

ELIZABETH LINDER

Burgess Publishing

A Little Lamb Book

All scripture quotations are taken from
the *King James Version* of the Bible.

7th Printing

The Little Red Hen
ISBN 0-89274-312-3

Published by Burgess Publishing, Inc.
P.O. Box 520
Broken Arrow, OK 74013

Little Red Hen

a faith tale

Once upon a time, there was a Little Red Hen, who loved God with all of her heart.

She had asked Jesus to be her Lord, and wanted to please Him from the start!

That if thou shalt confess with thy mouth the Lord Jesus, and shalt believe in thine heart that God hath raised him from the dead, thou shalt be saved.

For with the heart man believeth unto righteousness; and with the mouth confession is made unto salvation.

Romans 10:9,10

She had three neighbors at the farm who were Christians, too.

They all went to church and heard the Word, but Little Red Hen did the things God said to do!

But whoso keepeth his word, in him verily is the love of God perfected: hereby know we that we are in him.

1 John 2:5

Little Red Hen read the Bible each day.

"Who would like to read with me?" she asked her friends.

"Not I," said Mr. Duck. "I'm taking a trip to town."

"Not I," said Mrs. Cat. "I am going to lie down."

"Not I," grumbled Mr. Pig. **"I don't have time!"**

So she read the Word anyway!

My son, attend to my words; incline thine ear unto my sayings.
Let them not depart from thine eyes; keep them in the midst of thine heart.

Proverbs 4:20

My son, keep my words, and lay up my commandments with thee.

Proverbs 7:1

The Little Red Hen loved to pray.

"Would you like to pray also?" she asked her friends.

"Not I," said Mr. Duck. "I don't have a need."

"Not I," said Mrs. Cat. "I have too many kittens to feed."

"Not I," grumbled Mr. Pig. **"I don't have time."**

But Little Red Hen kept right on praying!

Pray without ceasing.
1 Thessalonians 5:17

Little Red Hen was very sad because she knew her friends were missing God's best.

They were too lazy to do the Word of God and put it to the test!

When any one heareth the word of the kingdom, and understandeth it not, then cometh the wicked one, and catcheth away that which was sown in his heart. This is he which received seed by the way side.

Matthew 13:19

I know, she thought, *I will have a Bible study and help them learn the Word.*

"Will you come?" she asked them hopefully.

"Not I," said Mr. Duck. "I just want to have fun."

"Not I," said Mrs. Cat. "I am going to visit my son."

"Not I," grumbled Mr. Pig. **"I don't have time."**

Go ye therefore, and teach all nations, baptizing them in the name of the Father, and of the Son, and of the Holy Ghost:
Matthew 28:19,20

All this time the Little Red Hen took very good care of her family.
She spent plenty of time with them and kept her house clean, you see.

God helped the Little Red Hen with everything she did.
She even trusted God to help her raise her kids!

She looketh well to the ways of her household, and eateth not the bread of idleness.
Her children arise up, and call her blessed; her husband also, and he praiseth her.

Proverbs 31:27,28

Little Red Hen knew that the winter snow was coming.

But her trust was in the Word, and she used her head!

She wanted to prepare her home with straw to keep it warm, and gather lots of food to keep her family fed.

She stretcheth out her hand to the poor; yea, she reacheth forth her hands to the needy.

She is not afraid of the snow for her household: for all her household are clothed with scarlet.

Proverbs 31:20,21

Then Little Red Hen thought of something she could do . . .

I will help my neighbors prepare their homes, and they can help me prepare mine, too!

Therefore all things whatsoever ye would that men should do to you, do ye even so to them: for this is the law and the prophets.

Matthew 7:12

"Would you like for me to help you prepare your house for winter?" she asked. "If we worked together, it would be much easier."

"Not I," said Mr. Duck. "I'm too old."
"Not I," said Mrs. Cat. "I never get cold."
"Not I," grumbled Mr. Pig. **"I don't have time."**

So Little Red Hen went home and did it all by herself!

Give her of the fruit of her hands; and let her own works praise her in the gates.

Proverbs 31:31

When winter came, the snow was piled up very high.

Little Red Hen was warm and cozy, and her house was very dry.

But deep inside she felt so sad because she knew her friends were cold. And she thought of poor Mr. Duck who was getting very old!

Then she had a wonderful idea . . .

If a man say, I love God, and hateth his brother, he is a liar: for he that loveth not his brother whom he hath seen, how can he love God whom he hath not seen?

1 John 4:20

Little Red Hen ran out into the deep snow and called her neighbors together.

"Will you come into my warm house and stay for the winter?" she asked. "I have more than enough room for you all."

"I will!" said Mr. Duck.
"I will!" said Mrs. Cat.
"I will, too!" said Mr. Pig in his nicest tone of voice.

But whoso hath this world's good, and seeth his brother have need, and shutteth up his bowels of compassion from him, how dwelleth the love of God in him?

1 John 3:17

All winter long, Little Red Hen taught her neighbors God's Word.

She prayed with them and shared the faith of God that she had heard.

Hereby perceive we the love of God, because he laid down
his life for us: and we ought to lay down our lives for the brethren.
1 John 3:16

After that winter, Mr. Duck and Mrs. Cat and Mr. Pig were not lazy Christians anymore.

They did *all* that God's Word said to do.

God blessed them; and if you are a doer of the Word, He will bless you, too!

If ye be willing and obedient, ye shall eat the good of the land.

Isaiah 1:19